SOLOMON
THE RUSTY NAIL

WILLIAM STEIG

FARRAR · STRAUS · GIROUX · NEW YORK

To the latest bunch:
Alicia, Charlotte, Curran, Evan, Geneva,
Georgia, Kate, Maggie, William

Copyright © 1985 by William Steig
All rights reserved
Library of Congress catalog card number: 85-81024
Published simultaneously in Canada by Collins Publishers, Toronto
Color separations by Offset Separations Corp.
Printed in the United States of America by Eastern Press, Inc.
Bound by A. Horowitz and Sons
Designed by Atha Tehon
First edition, 1985

Solomon was an ordinary rabbit, except for one thing: anytime he wanted to, he could turn into a rusty nail. How did he discover he had this gift?

He was sitting on the bench by his house one day, just gazing at the world, when he happened to scratch his nose and wiggle his toes at exactly the same time. And zingo! just like that, he became something hard and tiny.

He could still hear though he had no ears, and see though he had no eyes, but he couldn't figure out what he had turned into until his mother came out to sweep up. "What is this rusty nail doing on the bench?" she said, and chucked him in the trash can.

He couldn't cry out "Mom, it's me!" He had no way of making a sound. Naturally, he began to worry. What would become of him? Would he wind up at the town dump with the rest of the garbage, and stay there forever? Or what? "I don't belong in here with this junk," he said to himself. "I'm no nail, I'm a rabbit!"

The moment he thought those words, he was a rabbit again. In a daze, he climbed out of the trash can, went behind the toolshed, and sat down on the solid ground. Did what just happened really happen? It did. Dare he try to make it happen again?

He dared—over and over, until he was sure he could always do it. When he scratched his nose and wiggled his toes, he became a rusty nail. And when he thought "I'm no nail, I'm a rabbit," he was a rabbit.

His first idea was to show his family what a prize pazoozle of a rabbit he was. But then he decided to keep his secret secret.

At supper that night, his father, his mother, his two brothers, his sister chomped away at their chard and carrots. Did any of them even begin to realize who was sitting at their table? Not a one! Solomon had to smile.

At bedtime, he slipped under his quilt and turned into a rusty nail. And when his mother came to kiss him good night, there was no one there to kiss. "Where are you, son?" she called. "Here in bed! Where else?" he answered, popping into view. "What's going on here?" his mother asked herself on the way downstairs.

Starting the next day, he began mystifying his friends and family with odd disappearances. No matter how they searched, they could never find him.

Then that tricky rascal would turn up out of nowhere, looking smug and innocent.

His grandma said, and she wasn't the only one, "I can't figure that child out. First he's here, then he's there, then he isn't anywhere!" Solomon was proud to be the cause of all this confusion.

But after a while he tired of his trick and forgot it. Butterflies became his chief interest; he collected them. And he got so good at Parcheesi, he could even beat his father.

One day during summer vacation, Solomon was out in the hills chasing butterflies. He was just about to bag a rare one when he heard an ugly voice snarl: "Freeze! Up with your paws!" Solomon was so startled he dropped his net and his specimen box.

Right behind him, flashing a long knife, stood a one-eyed cat. "Keep reaching and start marching," the cat commanded.

Solomon obeyed. As he marched along in front of the knife, it occurred to him that he didn't have much longer to live. *Not much longer to live?* He broke for freedom, the dangerous cat at his scut.

But he couldn't keep running forever. WAIT! What about the old nail trick? Would it still work?

He dived behind a tree, scratching his nose and wiggling his toes; and when the cat zipped in after him, there was no Solomon. Nothing but trampled grass, a stone, and a rusty nail.

Solomon's not being where he just went discombobulated the cat. He kept circling that tree, clockwise, counterclockwise, and otherwise, trying to find his rabbit. He finally staggered off, feeling brainsick.

"I'm safe!" thought Solomon, and he returned to rabbithood. But he did it too soon. The cat turned around for one last look, spotted him, and raced right back. Poor Solomon had to change into a nail again—at the very toes of his enemy.

"Neat trick!" the cat said, and he headed home with Solomon in his pocket.

"Guess what I've got!" he announced to his wife, prancing into the parlor. "A plump young bunny for a savory stew."

He laid the rusty nail on a doily.

"*This* is a plump young bunny?" she said. "Are you sure, Ambrose?"

"Yes, Clorinda. This isn't really a nail, it's a rabbit. As soon as it stops pretending, presto chango, we'll have us a meal." And he told his goggle-eyed wife about the strange events of that morning.

The cats had a cage where they kept their victims until they were needed for the table. Clorinda put the precious nail inside and Ambrose padlocked the door. Now all they had to do was wait for Solomon to show up and turn him into Hasenpfeffer.

They decided to take turns keeping an eye on the cage, but of course Solomon knew just what was going on. He had no intention of serving as dinner for two stupid cats. He made up his mind to remain a nail for as long as he had to.

Ambrose and Clorinda watched and waited. When they were both snoring away in the next room, Solomon would quietly become himself and try to bend the bars or force the lock. But that didn't get him anywhere.

After three long weeks, the cats were out of patience. Clorinda began to suspect that her husband had made some kind of mistake. "Ambrose," she said at last, "are you absolutely, indelibly convinced that this sliver of metal is a real live rabbit?"

"Pussykins," he retorted, "if I'm a real cat, as I suspect I am, then this thing's a genuine rabbit."

"Prove it!" she said.

This tactless suggestion made Ambrose boil over. He unlocked the cage, hauled out the nail, and screamed, "Quit the hanky-panky, you stubborn piece of junk! Turn back into a bunny, at once!" Solomon chose not to.

Ambrose booted the door open and rushed outside. "Hurrah, I win!" thought Solomon. "He's going to throw me away!" But no. Ambrose grabbed a hammer and—bang! bang! bang!—he pounded Solomon into the side of the house and ran off raving.

"Tonight's the night!" thought Solomon, and as soon as the cats were asleep, he said the magic words to himself. He said them again and again, but every time he started to swell up with life, the wood he was in restrained him.

"Must I stay locked in this prison until it rots and caves in and releases me? That could take a hundred years. Would I still be alive then?" he wondered. "Do nails die?"

Day followed day over the mountain. To while away the time, Solomon took to counting—up to a million, a billion, a zillion.

Sometimes the world looked so beautiful he felt satisfied just being a tiny part of it, even embedded in wood. Mostly, though, he longed to be back home with his family.

How his poor parents must be suffering, he thought, not knowing what had become of him. How miserable they must be without their child.

Ambrose would often stare at him with disgust, but Solomon didn't mind. It made him feel less lonesome.

Once, Clorinda looked at him with such pity it made him feel like crying. But she was only thinking what a pity it was for a perfectly good dinner to be stuck in the wall.

One day, Ambrose was out in the back yard piddling around. He lit his pipe, then tossed the match aside, and before he knew it, the dry leaves on the ground were ablaze and flames were scurrying up the side of the house.

He was beating at the flames with his hat when Clorinda crashed through
the door, shrieking "I'm incinerated!" Together they ran for help.

When the flames reached Solomon, he first felt feverish, and then, though he couldn't even budge, he felt terribly alive, inspired, bright and central like the sun itself.

A gang of neighbors arrived, and in a jiffy they were passing buckets of water up from the pond and sloshing them at the house. But the fire insisted on finishing its job.

The house crumpled in a stuttering of sparks and was soon nothing but smoking embers and scattered nails—one of which was Solomon. He had reveled in being red-hot, and now, as the wretched company of cats departed, he enjoyed cooling off.

With the cats out of sight, Solomon resumed his natural form. At last! He took a deep breath and did a whooping backward somersault. Then he went tripping home.

His heartbroken family had found his net and his specimen box, and were sure he had been done in by some cruel carnivore. It was almost too much for them when Solomon, as alive as possible, came bursting into the house. After the shouting and the leaping, there was no end of hugging and kissing.

When things settled down, Solomon told them his story and finally revealed his secret. He turned into a rusty nail right in front of everyone, then back into their own dear Solomon.

They begged him never to do it again.
Except, of course, if he absolutely had to.